Mrs Lather's Laundry

Ahlberg & Amstutz

PUFFIN

PUFFIN BOOKS

UK | USA | Canada | Ireland | Australia
India | New Zealand | South Africa

Puffin Books is part of the Penguin Random House group of companies
whose addresses can be found at global.penguinrandomhouse.com.

www.penguin.co.uk   www.puffin.co.uk   www.ladybird.co.uk

First published in hardback by Viking and in paperback by Puffin Books 1981
This edition published 2016

001

Printed in China
A CIP catalogue record for this book is available from the British Library

ISBN: 978–0–141–36995–2

All correspondence to:
Puffin Books, Penguin Random House Children's
80 Strand, London WC2R 0RL

Monday was a bad day
in Mrs Lather's Laundry.
Mr Lather was having trouble
with the ironing.

Miss Lather and Master Lather
were having a tug of war
with the washing.

Mrs Lather was going crazy.
"If I wash one more sock,
I will go off my head!" she said.
"I am sick of socks.
I hate them!"

After that Mr Lather put a notice
in the laundry window.
It said:

Tuesday was another bad day
in Mrs Lather's Laundry.
Mr Lather was having trouble
with a sheet.

The children were playing
hide-and-seek in the washing.
They were playing tennis too.

Mrs Lather was going crazy again.
"If I wash one more vest,
I will go off my head!" she said.
"I am sick of vests.
I hate them!"
After that Mr Lather put another
notice in the window.
It said:

WE WASH ANYTHING
EXCEPT SOCKS AND VESTS

Then Mrs Lather said,
"And no pairs of pants either!
Or shirts or dresses!
Or table-cloths!
Or hankies!
I am sick of all of them.
I hate them!"
After that the children put
a notice in the window.
It said:

WE WASH ANYTHING

EXCEPT LAUNDRY

Wednesday was a *quiet* day
in Mrs Lather's Laundry.

But Thursday was a surprising day!
First a customer came in with a baby.
"We do not wash baby-clothes,"
said Mrs Lather.
"I do not want you to wash his clothes,"
said the customer.
"I want you to wash him!"
"Oh!" said Mrs Lather.
And she washed the baby.

After that more customers
came in with their babies.
There were rich customers
and poor customers;
old customers and young customers.
There was a big customer
with a little baby.
There was a little customer
with a big baby.

And there were lots more
customers besides.

At first Mrs Lather washed the babies
and was very happy.
"I like washing babies," she said.
"I love them!"

But by the end of the day
she was sick of them.
And a notice in the window said:
WE WASH ANYTHING
EXCEPT LAUNDRY AND BABIES

Friday was another surprising day
in Mrs Lather's Laundry.
A customer came in with a baby
and a dog.
"We do not wash babies,"
said Mrs Lather.
"I do not want you to wash the baby,"
said the customer.
"I want you to wash the dog!"
"Oh!" said Mrs Lather.

And she washed the dog.
After that, more customers
came with their dogs.
There were big dogs and little dogs;
long dogs and short dogs;
happy dogs and sad dogs;
black, brown and spotty dogs.

And lots more besides.

At first Mrs Lather washed the dogs.
Then she got sick of them,
and Mr Lather washed them.
Then he got sick of them,

and the children washed them.
By the end of the day
the notice in the window said:
WE WASH ANYTHING
EXCEPT LAUNDRY,
BABIES AND DOGS

Saturday was the worst day of all
in Mrs Lather's Laundry.
Mrs Lather washed:

I want you to wash me

a tramp,

a car,

a football team –
and an elephant!

The elephant was from a circus.
Mr Lather and the children
washed the elephant too.
When they got sick of it –
the elephant washed them!

Sunday was a *good* day
in Mrs Lather's Laundry.
The notice in the window said:

CLOSED

When Monday came round again,
Mrs Lather was feeling cheerful.
"Will you be going crazy today, Mum?"
the children said.
"No," said Mrs Lather.
"I feel cheerful now."
She began to laugh.
"After all – *what could be worse
than an elephant?*"

The End